Little One,
We Knew
You'd
Come

Little One,
We Knew You'd Come

By Sally Lloyd-Jones

Illustrated by Jackie Morris

 LITTLE, BROWN AND COMPANY

New York ∾ Boston ∾ London

First Edition: October 2006

Little, Brown and Company

1271 Avenue of the Americas, New York, NY 10020
Visit our Web site at www.lb-kids.com

Library of Congress Cataloging-in-Publication Data

Jones, Sally Lloyd.
  Little one, we knew you'd come / by Sally Lloyd-Jones ; illustrated by Jackie Morris.
    p. cm.
  ISBN-10: 0-316-52391-7 / ISBN-13: 978-0-316-52391-2
  1. Jesus Christ—Nativity—Juvenile literature. I. Morris, Jackie. II. Title.
  BT315.3.J66 2006
  232.92—dc22   2005024661

10 9 8 7 6 5 4 3 2 1

SC

Manufactured in China

The illustrations for this book were done in watercolor and gold leaf,
on Arches 140-lb hot-pressed paper.
The text and display type were set in Papyrus.

For Harry, Eleanor, Olivia,
Jonathan, and Emily—
I'm so glad you came!
—S.L.J.

To Kath and Ella
And to mothers everywhere
—J.M.

Little one,
    we knew you'd come.

We hoped. We dreamed. We watched for you.
We counted the days till you were due.
We waited. How we longed for you,

And the day that you were born.

Little one,
    we knew you'd come.

It was late at night. The time had come.
The time for you to come, my love.
You'll be here soon. We're ready for you,

And the day that you were born.

Little one,
        we knew you'd come.

By silver stars and golden moon,
At break of dawn, you came.
Kiss your nose, those tiny toes,

On the day that you were born.

Little one,
     we knew you'd come.

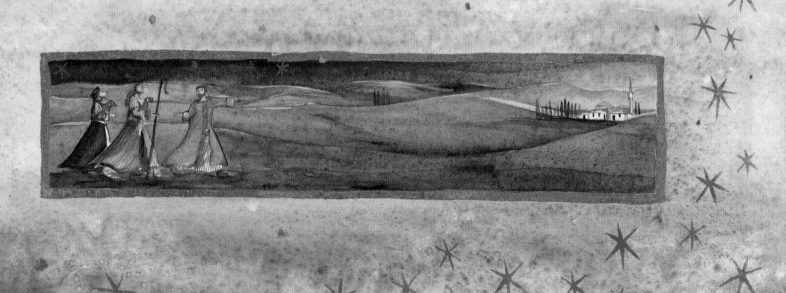

People were sleeping. We didn't care.
Good news, we sang, our baby is here!
Our baby has come, our darling one,

Oh, the day that you were born.

Little one,
   we knew you'd come.

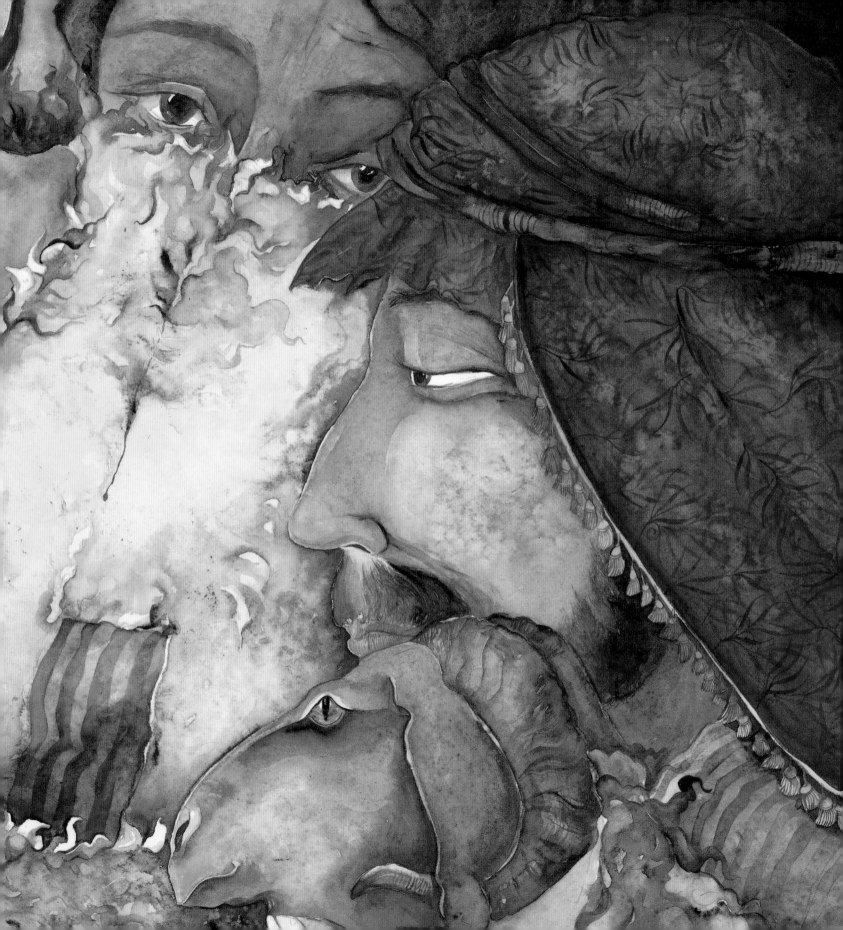

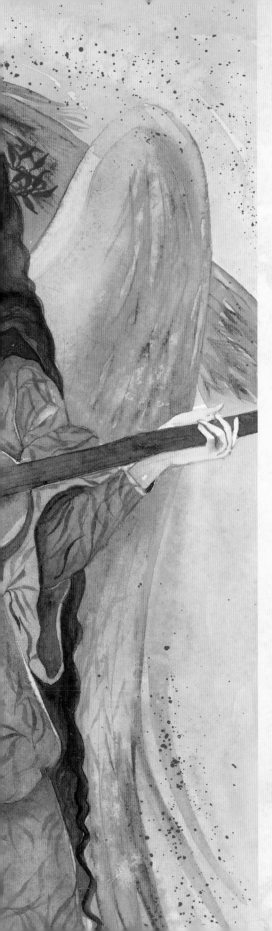

Kiss and cuddle and love the baby.
Scoop that baby up,
And softly sing a lullaby,

On the day that you were born.

Little one . . .

. . . we knew you'd come.

And every year, we remember you,
Our miracle child, our dreams come true.
Oh, how we thank Heaven for you,

And the day that you were born.

Little one,
we're so glad you've come!